The Sword in the Tree

by CLYDE ROBERT BULLA

Illustrated by PAUL GALDONE

SCHOLASTIC BOOK SERVICES

NEW YORK · LONDON · RICHMOND HILL, ONTARIO

For Dick

2nd printing .... December 1965

Printed in the U.S.A.

Contents

Weldon Castle

The boy sat up in bed. A sound in the night had wakened him.

His room was so dark he could see nothing, but he could hear steps outside his door. He held his breath and listened.

"Shan!" said a voice.

He let his breath go. It was his mother, calling his name.

"Yes?" he said. "What is it?"

Lady Marian came into the room. She had a candle in her hand, and the light moved over the stone walls.

"Shan, I'm glad to find you here," she said. "I was afraid you had gone with your father."

"Where has my father gone?" asked Shan.

"One of the servants just wakened him and they went away together," she said. "I heard them speak of a wounded knight."

"A *wounded* knight?" said Shan.

"Yes," said Lady Marian. "Shan, what does it mean? Is someone making war on us? Are there enemy soldiers outside?"

"Don't be afraid, Mother," said Shan. "Our good King Arthur has beaten all our enemies. And even if there *were* enemies, we would be safe here. There is no stronger castle in England than ours."

He went to the window. A light was moving in the courtyard below.

"Mother, I'm going down there," he said.

"I don't think you should go," said Lady Marian.

"No one is fighting," he said. "There's nothing to be afraid of."

Shan put on his clothes; then he ran down the stairs and into the courtyard. There was a light near the castle gate. He went toward it.

At the gate he found his father. Some of the servants were there too. One of them had a lighted torch in his hand.

"Father— " Shan stopped. On the stones at his father's feet lay a man. A long black beard hid his face. Two of the servants were taking off his armor.

"Who is he?" asked Shan.

"No one knows," said his father. "He pounded on the gate. We let him in, and he fell in a faint."

"My lord, I have found his wound," said one of the servants.

Shan's father looked at the wound in the man's side. "Bring him into the castle at once," he said.

The servants lifted the wounded man and carried him into a bedroom in the castle.

"Has he lost much blood?" asked Shan.

"I think so," said his father. "The wound is deep."

"Shall I bring Nappus?" asked Shan.

"Nappus?"

"Yes. Nappus is a man of magic. He can make the knight well."

"Poor Nappus." Shan's father shook his head. "He knows no magic. But he was once the best of doctors."

"He is still the best of doctors," said Shan.

"Remember how he took the fishbone from your throat? Remember how he bound up my arm when it was broken?"

"Yes, yes," said his father. "Go and bring him if you wish."

Shan took a lighted torch from one of the servants and ran out across the courtyard. He opened a door in the castle wall. It was the door to Nappus' room.

Nappus was sleeping, with his cloak over his head. Shan touched him. Nappus looked out from under the cloak.

He was a small man. His hair was white. He could neither hear nor speak, but his eyes' were keen and bright.

"There is a wounded knight in the castle," said Shan. "Come and dress his wound."

Nappus watched Shan's lips, reading the words. He nodded to show that he understood. From a box in a corner he took some jars and bottles, and tied them up in a cloth.

Shan led the way to the castle. Nappus knelt by the wounded man. He washed the wound and

dressed it. He opened the man's mouth and poured a little red wine down his throat.

The man moved. His eyes opened, and he looked at Nappus. "Lord Weldon!" he said in a whisper. "Where is Lord Weldon?"

Shan's father came forward. "I am Lord Weldon. You are safe in Weldon Castle."

The wounded man tried to lift himself. "My brother!" he said. Then he fell back and was still.

Shan's father bent over the man and looked into his face. He cried out, "Lionel!" His voice shook with excitement. Then he turned to Shan. "This knight is my brother; I am sure of it. Shan, this is your Uncle Lionel. After these many years, your Uncle Lionel has come home!"

Uncle Lionel

Shan had heard many tales of his uncle. Now he wanted to hear more. "Tell me about my Uncle Lionel," he said to his father.

"Wait until he is strong," said Lord Weldon, "and he will tell you himself."

But Shan was impatient. He asked his mother, "Will *you* tell me about my uncle?"

"I never knew him well," she said, "He sailed from England long before you were born. He was wild when he was a boy. He was never a kind and gentle knight, and he was never as brave as your father."

"Did he live here at Weldon Castle?" asked Shan.

"No," said Lady Marian. "He had a castle of his own, but he sold it and quickly spent the money Then he went away to France and Spain and other far places."

"Do you think he will tell me about those far places?" asked Shan.

"He may," said his mother, "when he is strong again."

Every day Shan sat for a while by Lionel's bed. Most of the time his uncle slept. When he looked about him, his eyes were bright with fever and he knew no one.

But one morning, when he awoke, the fever was gone from his eyes. He looked at Shan.

"Why do you sit there?" he asked.

Shan looked at him in surprise.

"Why do you sit and look at me?" cried Lionel. "Speak, you young dog!"

Shan jumped to his feet. "I am no dog. I am the son of Lord Weldon."

"You lie! My brother has no son."

"I do *not* lie, and you have no right to say so!" Shan turned and walked out of the room. On the stairs he met his father.

"I'll sit with my uncle no more," he said.

"Why?" asked Lord Weldon. "What has he done?"

"He called me a dog," said Shan. "He said I was no son of yours."

"He said those things to you? Then my brother must be better," said Lord Weldon, and he ran upstairs.

Shan went outside. He was so angry, he felt warm all over. No one had ever talked to him before as his uncle had talked to him just now.

He went to the stone trough near the castle gate. It was the trough where the horses were watered. He put his head down into it and let the water cool his face.

He saw old Nappus sitting by the wall. Shan started across the courtyard to sit beside him, but before he got there someone called his name.

It was Lord Weldon calling from the window of Lionel's room. "Come, Shan!"

Shan did not want to go, but he knew he must obey his father. He walked slowly back toward the castle.

Inside he found his father and Lionel laughing and talking together.

"This is a great day for us all," said Lord Weldon. "Your uncle can sit up. He can talk and laugh again. See how much better he is?"

"Yes, Father," said Shan.

"You must not be angry at the things he said. That was only a joke."

"Yes," said Lionel. "It was only a joke. Take my hand."

Shan went to the bed and took his uncle's hand.

"We must be friends," said Lionel. "Here, let me look at you. How old are you?"

"Eleven, sir," said Shan.

"And what do you wish to be when you are a man?"

"A knight," said Shan.

"Good!" said Lionel. "I can teach you all the things a knight should know. How to ride, how to use a lance and sword — "

"My father is teaching me those things," said Shan.

"I'll teach you even more," said Lionel. "We can start today."

Lord Weldon spoke up. "No, not today. Remember your wound."

"Ah yes, my wound. I'd like to have my hands on the dog who gave it to me!" said Lionel.

He told them what had happened. "Late in the evening I was riding toward Weldon Castle. In the woods three robbers set upon me. One of them wounded me with a knife. They stole my purse, my sword and shield, and my horse."

"There are many robbers in the land," said Lord Weldon. "It is not safe to ride in the woods alone."

"No gold, no horse, no sword or shield," said Lionel. "What a poor knight am I!"

"Not poor at all," said Lord Weldon. "You are with your own people again. You have a home with us."

"My good brother," said Lionel. "How can I ever thank you?" And he bowed his head over his brother's hand.

The Oak Tree

The next day Lionel asked to be taken outside.

"I want to sit in the shade of the great oak tree," he said.

The oak tree stood in the castle garden. There were some who said it was the oldest tree in all England. Ever since Shan was a small boy, he had liked to climb it. High in its trunk he had found a hollow so large that he could nearly get inside it.

"I fear the oak will die, with such a large hollow in its trunk," Lord Weldon had said.

But the tree was still strong and green, and each spring it put out new leaves and branches.

Four servants carried Lionel, bed and all, into the garden. They put him down under the oak tree.

"Stay with him until I come back," Lord Weldon told Shan.

"Where are you going, Father?" asked Shan.

"It is time for me to ride through my lands," said Lord Weldon. "I want to talk with the farmers and see how the crops are growing."

One of the things Shan liked best was riding with his father. "I wish I could go," he said.

"So do I," said his father, "but your uncle doesn't like being left alone."

So Shan stayed with his uncle.

"Is your father gone much of the time?" asked Lionel.

"Only when he rides out through his lands," said Shan.

"Doesn't he ever go away to war?"

"There is no war in England. These are times of peace," said Shan. "For many years we have had no prisoners in the dungeon under our castle."

"No prisoners? Then what do you do with your dungeon?"

"Nothing. I wish my father would have it filled with earth and stones. It is such an ugly place, with no window for the sun to shine in."

"You had better keep your dungeon. You may have need of it." Suddenly Lionel sat up straight. "Look! What is that old man doing here?" He shouted in a loud voice, "Go!"

The old man was bending over a rosebush. He did not look up.

Lionel turned red with anger. "Bring me a stone to throw. I'll have him out in a hurry."

"You must do him no harm," said Shan. "That is Nappus."

"Nappus? Who is Nappus?"

"He is the one who cared for you and dressed your wound. He has a right to come to this garden. He finds snails and herbs here for his medicines."

"But why did he not speak when I spoke to him?"

"He could not hear you," said Shan. "Years ago he was caught in the woods by a storm. He stood under a tree, and the tree was struck by lightning. After that day, Nappus could not hear nor speak. But he is very wise. There are some who say he is a man of magic."

"Then I would do him no harm," said Lionel. "It is good luck to have such a man about the castle. Old man!" he called. "You may stay if you like . . . Oh, I forgot. He cannot hear me."

Shan went to Nappus. He looked among the rosebushes and found two big brown snails. He put them in Nappus' hand.

Nappus smiled and nodded. Then he saw Lionel, and the smile left his face. He turned and went quickly away.

"He is a strange old man," said Lionel.

"He knows many things," said Shan. "He helped make my sword."

"Have you a sword of your own?" asked Lionel.

"Yes, I have," said Shan.

"Bring it here," said Lionel.

Shan went to the great hall of the castle. The armor was kept there in wooden chests. On the walls were lances, bows and arrows, swords, and shields. Shan climbed up on one of the chests and took down his sword and shield. They were smaller than those used by the men.

He put on his belt and scabbard, and slid the sword into the scabbard. Then he took up the shield and ran out into the garden.

"Do you practice with these?" asked Lionel.

"Every day," said Shan, "and with a crossbow too. And I practice climbing and riding and jumping."

"Draw your sword," said Lionel.

Shan drew his sword from the scabbard.

"Faster!" said Lionel.

Shan tried again. He drew the sword as quickly as he could.

"That is better," said Lionel. "Now I'll see you ride."

Shan went to the stables. "Bring me my horse," he told a groom.

The groom brought the horse to the garden. Shan got into the saddle. The groom handed up his shield.

"Now," said Lionel, "ride to the end of the garden walk and back — and be quick."

Shan put his heels to the horse's sides, and the horse was off. He rode to the end of the walk. He turned and rode back.

"You sit well enough in the saddle," said Lionel, "but your turn was too slow. Try again. Jerk the reins when you turn your horse. Jerk as hard as you can and bring his feet off the ground."

"I'll not do that," said Shan.

"What!" said Lionel.

"It isn't good to jerk a horse on a turn," said Shan. "A strong pull is better and faster."

"Are you telling *me* how to turn a horse?"

"I ride as my father taught me."

"It's time I taught you a real lesson!" Lionel tried to get to his feet.

"No!" said Shan. "You'll hurt yourself."

Lionel fell back on the bed. "Get out of my sight!" he shouted.

As Shan rode out of the garden, he heard his uncle still shouting, "Out of my sight! Out of my sight, you bold brat!"

The Hunt

After that day, Lionel said no more about teaching Shan to ride or use a sword.

When his wound had healed, he took long rides beyond his brother's lands. Often he brought strange men back with him.

Some of them he had known in France or Spain,

he said. Others he had met along the road. Night after night they came to the castle. They sat in the great hall, singing and eating and drinking.

"I do not like these strange, rough men," said Lady Marian.

"These men are my brother's friends," said Lord Weldon.

"I wish you would send them away," said Lady Marian, "and send your brother with them."

"Send my brother away?" said Lord Weldon. "I could not do that."

"Will he always be here?" she asked. "Will he and his friends always be at our table, eating our food and drinking our wine?"

"My brother is well and strong now," said Lord Weldon. "He will soon ride away to look for new adventures."

But the weeks went by, and Lionel stayed.

One autumn morning he and some of his friends went fox hunting. Lord Weldon went with them.

From his window in the castle, Shan watched them ride away. Each had a hunting knife at his side, and some had spears and bows and arrows.

Dogs were barking and running in and out among the horses.

No one had asked Shan to go, but he did not mind. He liked to hunt with his father, but he had no wish to go with Lionel and his friends.

He went down to the great hall. From a shelf he took the long box in which his father's sword was kept.

Shan was sure it was the most beautiful sword in the world. The blade was of fine blue steel. The hilt was of gold, set with small red stones. When he took the sword from the box, the stones flashed in the light.

Long ago Shan had asked his father, "May I be the one to care for your sword?"

His father had told him, "Yes, my son, because some day it will be yours."

Shan rubbed the blade with oil so that the steel would not rust. He rubbed the hilt with a soft cloth until the gold was clean and bright.

While he worked, the great hall began to grow dark. He put the sword away.

He went outside and looked at the sky. It was

dark with clouds, and a few drops of rain were falling.

His mother called to him from the castle, "Come out of the rain, Shan."

He went inside. He climbed the stairs to his mother's room.

Lady Marian was sitting by the window. "Now are you glad you did not go on the hunt?"

"Yes, Mother," he said. "It is a poor day for hunting."

"Your father will come home wet and cold," she said. "We must have a good fire ready for him."

Shan was at the window. "I think I see the men coming now."

"Oh no. It is too soon."

"But I see men on horseback."

They looked out into the rain.

"Yes," she said. "Now I see them."

They watched as the men came nearer.

"Where is my father?" asked Shan.

"I do not see him," said his mother, "but I see your uncle."

"There is one horse without a rider," said Shan.

"Yes," she said, "and your uncle is leading it."

"That is my father's horse!" said Shan.

"But your father —! Shan, he is not with the others!"

She ran down the stairs and into the courtyard.

Shan ran after her. They were waiting in the rain when Lionel and his friends rode up to the castle.

"Where is my father?" asked Shan.

The men looked at one another. One by one they rode away until only Lionel was left.

Shan's mother spoke to him. "Where is my lord?"

"I bring sad news," he said.

"What news?" she asked.

"Do you know the quicksand on this side of the river?" said Lionel. "My brother rode into it. His horse saved himself, but my brother was lost. We saw him go down in the quicksand. We were too late to save him."

Lady Marian's face was white. She started toward the castle, walking as if she could not see. Shan helped her across the courtyard and up the stairs to her room.

"Don't leave me," she said.

Lionel came up to the room. "Dear lady, what can I say? This is a terrible day for us all."

"Go away," she said. "Leave me alone with my son."

The Sword

For many days Lady Marian did not leave her room. She wanted no one near her except Shan. Every day someone from the kitchen left food outside the door. And every night firewood was brought to the room.

It was a time of fog and cold. Sometimes there was not enough wood to keep the room warm.

"I'll go tell them to bring more," Shan would say, and his mother would say, "Don't leave me, Shan. Stay with me. You are all I have now."

One night, as they sat by the fire, she said, "Hear the men singing and laughing below. They do not care how sad we are."

"Let me go speak to them," he said.

"No, don't leave me," she said.

"Mother, we cannot always stay in this room," said Shan. "Some day I must go out, and so must you."

She looked at him in surprise. "Yes, that is true," she said. "Go then."

He went down the stairs. Lionel and his friends were at the table in the great hall. Servants were bringing food and wine. They were servants Shan had never seen before.

He stood in the doorway. "Look, you!" he said. "This is a sad time for my mother and me. If you must make your noise, make it somewhere else."

Lionel set down his wine cup. "These are my friends," he said, "so take care how you speak to them."

"Take care how you speak to *me*," said Shan.

He went back to his mother. "There are strange faces here," he said. "I do not know what it means."

In the morning he went to the kitchen and the garden and the stables. Everywhere he went, he saw new faces. Most of the old servants were gone. New ones had taken their places.

Shan saw his uncle riding across the court-yard. He spoke to Lionel. "Who brought in new servants and sent the old ones away?"

"Some of my friends have come here to live," said Lionel. "They brought their own servants. We had no need of so many, and I sent some of the old ones away."

"Why did you not ask me first?"

"Why should I have asked you?"

"Now that my father is gone," said Shan, "*I* am Lord Weldon. *I* am master of the castle."

"You?" Lionel threw back his head and laughed. "You are a boy!"

He started to ride away. Shan saw that he wore a sword with a gold hilt. The hilt was set with red stones.

"Stop!" Shan cried. "Why do you wear that sword?"

"Why should I not wear it?" asked his uncle.

"It was my father's," said Shan. "Now it is mine."

"This is a sword for a man, not a boy. Out of my way!" Lionel rode off across the courtyard.

Shan looked after him. He said in a low voice, "The sword is not his. It is mine, and I'll have it back."

That night, when everyone else was in bed, Shan went down to the great hall. A fire still burned in the big fireplace. By its light he could see the room. On the wall behind his uncle's chair was the sword.

He took it down and put it back into its box. He looked about for a place to hide it. There was no place in the great hall.

He went out into the garden. His first thought was to bury the box in the ground. Then he

looked up at the oak tree and remembered the hollow in its trunk.

In the great hall he found a piece of rope and tied it to the box. With the rope about his shoulders and the box on his back, he climbed the oak tree. He found the hollow in the trunk.

There were sticks and leaves in the opening. He pulled them out and pushed the box inside. It fell softly into the hollow.

He climbed down. He felt his way through the quiet garden and into the castle.

In the morning Shan met his uncle in the courtyard.

"The sword!" cried Lionel, in a rage. "What have you done with the sword?"

"The sword is in a safe place," said Shan.

"Bring it to me. Bring it at once!"

"The sword is mine," said Shan.

Lionel lifted his hand as if to strike him. Shan did not move. Lionel let his hand fall to his side.

"Listen to what I say, and listen well," he said. "If the sword is not back in its place by tomorrow, I'll have you in the dungeon!"

"You forget that I am master here," said Shan, "and now I am going out to find our old servants and friends and bring them back."

He went to the stables. A stableman opened a window and looked out at him.

"Saddle a horse and bring it here to me," said Shan.

"I cannot, sir," said the man.

"You cannot?"

"No, sir," said the stableman. "Not until my master bids me to."

"*I* bid you to," said Shan. "*I* am your master."

"No, sir. My master is Lord Lionel." The man closed the window.

Shan was about to beat on the window and shout, "Bring me a horse, or I'll make you pay for this!" Then he looked up and saw Nappus by the castle wall. The old man looked at him and slowly shook his head.

Shan knew that the old man was trying to tell him something. He started over to the wall. Again Nappus shook his head, and he made a sign for Shan to go away.

Shan told his mother that night, as they sat by the fire, "Most of our old servants are gone, but Nappus is with us still."

"I am glad of that," she said.

"It may be that my uncle is afraid to send Nappus away," said Shan. "He thinks Nappus is a man of magic."

"Poor Nappus is no man of magic," said Lady Marian, "but he does know many things, and he is our friend. I wish we had more such friends."

"Listen!" said Shan. "Did you hear someone on the stairs?"

"No," she said.

"It may be my uncle, looking for the sword," he said.

"What sword?"

"The sword that was my father's," said Shan. "I have it hidden. My uncle says if I do not give it up, he will have me in the dungeon."

"Give him the sword," she said.

"I *never* will!" said Shan.

"But what if he takes you to the dungeon?"

"Listen!" said Shan again.

There was a soft knock at the door.

"If it is your uncle, give him the sword," she said in a whisper.

Shan opened the door. The man outside was not his uncle. It was Nappus.

Words in the Ashes

Nappus' cloak was wet from the fog. There were drops of water on his beard.

He looked quickly from Shan to Lady Marian. He knelt by the fire and raked some ashes out upon the hearth. With his fingers he made some marks in the ashes.

Shan and his mother bent over the hearth.

Nappus rubbed out the marks and made some more.

"What is he doing?" asked Shan.

"He is writing words in the ashes," said Lady Marian.

"Can you read them?" asked Shan.

"Yes," she whispered. "Oh, yes!"

She took up a candle and held it over the hearth. The candle shook in her hand.

It seemed a long time before Nappus was through writing in the ashes. When he stood up, he looked at Lady Marian.

She nodded. "Yes, I understand."

He knelt and kissed the hem of her dress. He threw his cloak about him. Like a shadow, he was gone.

Lady Marian sat down and put her hands over her face. "Oh, Shan, what shall we do now?"

"What were the words in the ashes?" he asked. "What did they say?"

"Shan, listen to me. Because Nappus cannot hear, most people think he cannot understand.

But he can look at their faces and read their lips. Today he read your uncle's lips as he talked to one of his friends—"

Her voice broke.

Shan bent over her. "Mother, what is it?"

"Your father did not die in the quicksand," she said. "He fell into a trap that was laid by your uncle."

Shan looked at her. He could not speak.

"Now," she said, "you and I are in the same danger."

"But *why*? What did my father do?" he cried. "What have *we* done?"

"Softly, Shan. Do you not see? With you and your father and me out of the way, your uncle will be lord of Weldon Castle."

He started to the door. She caught his arm. "Where are you going?"

"To settle with my uncle," he said.

"How can you settle with him? You cannot fight him and all his friends and their servants. Shan, there is only one way for us to save ourselves."

"What is that?" he asked.

"We must leave here. We must leave quickly."

"And give up our castle to my uncle?"

"If we stay, we cannot save our castle. If we go, we may save our lives. Do you understand?"

"I understand," he said.

She opened a chest and took out a cloak and a purse. "I have some money and my jewels," she said. "And here is the bread and cheese left from our supper."

"I have a little money," he said. He went to his room. From one of his chests he took a purse and a cloak. From another he took a knife, some string, and a tinderbox.

Back in his mother's room, he said, "I saw no one on the stairs. I think it is safe to go."

"The night watchmen are on the wall," she said.

"The fog is thick. The night watchmen cannot see us."

"Then let us go," she said.

They went down the stairs. She looked out into the night. "Can you see?" she asked.

"Only a little," he said.

They felt their way through the fog. They came to the castle gate. It was closed for the night.

Shan found the small door in the gate. He opened it. He helped his mother through.

They found the road and began to run. When they stopped for breath, Shan turned for a last look at the castle, but he could not see it. He could see only the night and the fog.

The Robbers

All night they walked. When morning came, they hid in the woods. They did not stop at any of the farms near the castle, for they knew that Lionel might find them there.

All day they hid. They ate the food that Lady Marian had brought from home. There was only a small piece of bread and a smaller piece of cheese.

At night they started on again. Once they heard horsemen on the road behind them. They hid by the roadside until the men went by.

"Do you think that was my uncle and his men?" asked Shan.

"I do not know," said his mother, "but I fear the roads are not safe for us, even at night. We had better take to the woods."

They walked through the woods. Slowly they made their way, until Lady Marian said, "I must rest."

They sat down on the roots of a tree. Shan felt the cold fog on his face. All about him he heard strange sounds. Some were the sounds of animals moving among the trees. He knew there were deer and foxes and rabbits in the woods. They would do no harm. But he knew there were wolves, too. A fire would keep them away, he thought.

He dug among the roots of the tree until he found dry leaves and sticks. From his purse he took his tinderbox. He struck a spark with the flint and steel. The spark fell into the tinder and caught fire. He lighted the dry leaves and sticks.

In a little while the fire was burning brightly. His mother held out her hands to it.

"It feels good," she said. "Now if only we had something to eat."

"I'll find something tomorrow." He sat down by her. "Mother, where are we going? What are we going to do?"

"The only plan I have is for us to go on — so far from Weldon Castle that your uncle can never find us," she said. "Then I hope we can find friends who will help us."

"I hope that will be soon," said Shan. "I am tired of hiding and running away." He leaned back against the tree.

"Go to sleep, Shan," she said.

"You sleep if you can," he said. "I'll stay awake and keep watch."

She lay down by the fire and was soon asleep.

Shan tried to keep watch, but he was very tired. He began to nod. Slowly his eyes went shut.

When he awoke, three strange men stood in the light of the fire. They were looking down on him and his mother. Their swords were drawn.

One of the men came closer. He wore a fine velvet hat with a feather. The rest of his clothes were in rags.

"Who are you?" he asked in a rough voice. "Why do you come here?"

Lady Marian woke and cried out.

Shan got to his feet. "My mother and I are going to the next town," he said. "We stopped here for rest and sleep."

"Are you alone?" asked the man.

"You can see we are alone," said Lady Marian.

"Stay and rest then," said the man. "But we'll have your purses before we go."

Lady Marian threw her purse at the man's feet. "You are brave men," she said, "to rob a woman and a boy."

"Hold your tongue." The robber said to Shan, "Quick, boy, your purse!"

Shan gave the robber his purse. "There is nothing much in it," he said. "Only a tinderbox, some string, and a few coins. Will you take the coins and leave me the rest?"

The robber looked into the purse.

"We have not had food for a long time," said Shan. "I need the string to make a trap to catch rabbits. I need the tinderbox so that we may have a fire."

The robbers went back into the shadows. They talked in low voices.

Shan saw one of them put something down on a stone. Then they disappeared into the woods.

Shan went to see what they had left. "Mother," he said, "here is my tinderbox and string!"

"The jewels and money are gone," she said.

"But here is something else," said Shan. "Look."

It was a loaf of bread.

"I want no gift from a robber," she said.

Shan broke the loaf in two and put half down beside her. He began to eat the other half.

"The bread is good," he said.

Lady Marian looked at the half-loaf beside her. She picked it up and tasted it.

"Yes, the bread *is* good," she said, "and I should not be so proud when I am hungry." She began to eat.

When they had eaten the loaf, Shan found more dry wood to burn. Then they lay down by the fire and rested until morning.

Magnus

They walked all morning. They waded across
a stream and pushed their way through vines and
bushes that tore their clothes.

"This is a strange place," said Lady Marian.
"See how thick and dark the woods are."

"I am glad they are thick and dark," said Shan. "My uncle can never find us here."

Shan saw how slow his mother's steps had grown. He knew that she was very tired.

He stopped under a tree and made her a bed of leaves. "Rest here, while I look for food."

She lay down. In a little while she was asleep.

Shan went on through the woods. From his purse he took the string he had brought from home. He began to make a rabbit trap out of it.

Then he had a better idea. He took out his knife and cut some branches off a tree. Quickly he made a bow and arrow.

He hid behind a tree and watched for a rabbit or a squirrel. There was a sound in the bushes. He set the arrow to the bowstring and waited.

Something came out of the bushes — something small and white, with soft brown eyes. It was a baby goat.

Shan put down his bow and arrow. The goat saw him and ran straight into his arms.

Shan laughed as he rubbed the baby goat's nose and ears. "I wouldn't hurt you," he said.

"You are someone's pet." With the goat in his
arms, he got to his feet.

"Stop, you!" said a voice.

Shan turned. There stood a boy and a dog.

The boy was as tall as Shan. He was dressed
in goatskins, and his long hair hung down over
his eyes. The dog was big and spotted. Its hair

hung down over its eyes too. Shan thought the boy and dog looked a little alike.

"What do you mean," said the boy, "trying to make off with my kid?"

Shan put the goat down. "I wasn't making off with him. I was going to show him to my mother."

"There's a fine story," said the boy. "Maybe you wanted to show him to all your brothers and sisters as well!"

He came up and gave Shan a push. Shan pushed him back. The dog began to bark.

The boy tried to catch Shan by the arms. He was strong, but he was slow. Shan bent low. He caught the boy around the legs and threw him to the ground.

The boy lay there on his back. With his mouth open in surprise, he looked up at Shan. "Eh! How did you do that?"

"Shall I do it again?" asked Shan.

"Don't trouble yourself," said the boy.

"Tell your dog to stop his noise," said Shan, "before he wakes my mother."

"Stop it, Tick," said the boy, and the dog stopped barking.

Shan went back to where he had left his mother. She was still sleeping.

The boy had followed him. "Who's that?" he asked.

"My mother," said Shan.

"And I thought it was just a big story you were giving me." The boy said softly, "She's beautiful as any queen."

"We've come a long way, and she isn't used to walking so far," said Shan. "I was trying to find her something to eat."

"Come home with me," said the boy. "We'll find food for the two of you."

"Where do you live?" asked Shan.

"See that path? Take it to the bottom of the hill, and there's the house," said the boy. "My father is a herdsman. He keeps a herd of goats and sheep, and my mother and I help him. You bring your mother. I'll run ahead and tell them, so everything will be ready." He ran away, with the dog and the white kid close behind him.

Shan wakened his mother. "I've met a boy, a herdsman's son," he said. "He has asked us to come to his home."

"Do you think it is safe?" she asked.

"I think so," he said.

They walked down the path. They came to the herdsman's house. It was a small house with walls of sticks and earth. Beside it was a barn, and all about the barn were pens for the sheep and goats.

The boy came down the path to meet them. He made a little bow to Shan's mother. "My father and mother both say you are welcome."

"Thank you," said Lady Marian. She and Shan went inside. They met Adam the herdsman and Phebe his wife.

"My son and I have had troubles, and we have nowhere to go," said Lady Marian. "If you will keep us here for a while, we will find some way to pay you."

"It is proud we are," said Adam the herdsman, "to have such a fine lady and her son under our roof."

Phebe put bread and cheese on the table. She said to the boy, "Run, Magnus, and bring fresh milk."

Magnus picked up a jug and ran outside.

"It will be a poor meal, I fear," said Phebe.

"It will be our best in many a day," said Lady Marian. And she said in a low voice to Shan, "These are kind, honest people. It was good luck that led us here."

A Promise

The fall rains passed, and the winter snows came. In the home of the herdsman, Shan and his mother were safe and warm.

Shan helped care for the herd. He took hay and water to the sheep and goats. Phebe made him goatskin clothes like Magnus'.

Every day he and Magnus went hunting. With their bows and arrows they brought down rabbits and squirrels. Once they brought down a red deer.

Sometimes Adam and the two boys cut wood for the fire. They hauled it to the house in a cart. Load after load they hauled, until there was a great pile of wood outside the door.

Shan and Magnus made wooden swords. When the day's work was done, they played they were knights. They used Phebe's iron pot lids for shields and fought battles in the snow.

"Some day I'm going to be a knight," said Shan. "I'll ride out with my sword and shield. I'll find people in trouble and help them."

"I'll be a herdsman like my father," said Magnus.

"Don't you want to ride out and have adventures?" asked Shan.

"You and I are not alike," said Magnus. "You were born to be a knight or a lord. I was born to work with the herds."

"Some day," said Shan, "I'm going back and

take Weldon Castle from my uncle. Some day, when I'm a knight."

"Eh! That's a long time to wait," said Magnus.

"Yes," said Shan. "A long time."

One evening a man came to the door of the herdsman's house. At first Shan and his mother were afraid he might be one of Lionel's men. They drew back from the firelight so that he could not see their faces.

But the man was only a hunter who had lost his way.

As they sat by the fire, he sang songs and told stories. He had been in every part of the land, and he liked to tell of the places he had seen.

"Have you been to Camelot?" asked Adam.

"That I have," said the hunter.

"Did you see King Arthur's castle?" asked Adam.

"That I did," said the hunter. "Its towers are the highest in Camelot."

"Did you see the King?" asked Magnus.

"No," said the hunter, "because I was not there on one of the special days."

"Are there special days," asked Phebe, "when people may see the King?"

"Yes," said the hunter. "Now that the wars are over, King Arthur has more time for the people. On two special days each month he opens his doors to them. They tell him their troubles. He listens and tries to help them."

"But is it not true," asked Phebe, "that only those who are rich may take their troubles to the King?"

"He listens to the rich and poor alike," said the hunter.

Shan looked at his mother. "Did you hear?" he whispered.

She did not answer.

The next day, after the hunter had gone, Shan said to his mother, "When shall we start to Camelot?"

"It is a long way," she said, "and I am not strong."

"Then I will go alone," said Shan.

"All the way to Camelot? You don't know what you are saying," said his mother. "No, Shan, you are all I have. I want no harm to come to you."

"What harm could come to me? I am quick and strong, and I am not afraid. I must tell the King of our troubles. I know he will help drive my uncle out of our castle."

"You are still a boy," she said. "Why do you think King Arthur would listen to you?"

"If he listens to rich and poor alike," said Shan, "then he will listen to me. Mother, will you let me go to Camelot to see the King?"

She said again, "You are still a boy."

Every day he asked her. Every day she shook her head.

Toward the end of spring, Adam spoke up for him. He said to Lady Marian, "If Shan goes, he should be on his way before winter comes again."

"It is a long way for a boy to go alone," she said.

"Shall I send my son to go with yours?" asked Adam.

"That is kind of you," she said, "but Magnus is no older than Shan."

"True," said Adam. "Still, they could look out for each other on the way. And here is something else that comes to mind. My neighbor, Twiggs, is loading a raft with hay. He is taking the hay down the river to Farol Castle. And Farol Castle is only two days' walk from Camelot."

"Magnus and I can ride down the river with Twiggs," said Shan. "Did you hear, Mother?"

"Yes, I heard," she said.

"You won't say no again, will you?" he asked.

"I can see you have made up your mind. I can see that you will never be happy until you go," she said. "Yes, you may go."

"Oh, thank you!" said Shan. "You won't be sorry."

"I hope not," she said.

"You won't be," he said. "I promise you, Mother!"

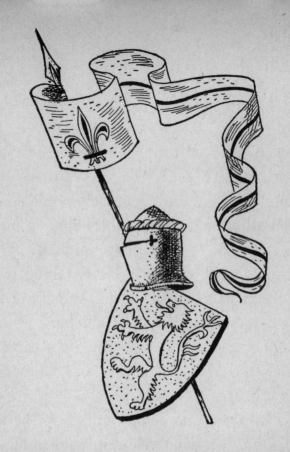

Camelot

It was early morning when Twiggs started down the river. His raft was piled high with clean, fresh hay. Shan and Magnus sat on top of the load. Twiggs stood on one side. With a long pole he pushed the raft away from the shore.

They floated slowly down the river. Sometimes Shan and Magnus lay back and looked at the sky. Sometimes they sat up and watched the woods and fields go by. Magnus had some wheat in his pocket. Now and then they chewed a little of it to keep from growing hungry.

Twiggs threw some string and two hooks of bone up to them. "See if you can catch some fish for supper," he said.

Shan and Magnus fished from the top of the load. They used bread for bait.

For a long time they caught nothing. Then they came to a pool full of fish. All the way across the pool they pulled out one fish after another.

At sundown Twiggs tied the raft to a tree, and they went ashore. Shan brought wood. Magnus built a fire. Twiggs cooked the fish in an iron pan.

After supper Magnus asked, "Are we going on now?"

"The night is too dark," said Twiggs. "I can't see to guide my raft. We will stay here till morning."

They made their beds in the hay. Long after

Twiggs and Magnus had gone to sleep, Shan lay awake. He looked at the stars. He listened to the night sounds — the hoot of an owl, the barking of foxes, the croaking of frogs along the river.

He thought of many things. He thought of his mother and father, and how happy they had been at Weldon Castle. He thought of his uncle. "He will pay for all he has done," said Shan to himself. "The King will help me, and my uncle will pay!"

The next day they came to Farol Castle. Just after sundown they tied up the raft near the walls.

A watchman called down, "Who is there?"

"Twiggs, with hay for your stables," Twiggs called back.

"Stay until morning," said the watchman. "The gate is closed for the night."

Once more Twiggs, Shan, and Magnus slept on the raft. Early in the morning two men came out of Farol Castle to help Twiggs unload the hay. Shan and Magnus took the road to Camelot.

When night came, they stopped at a house in the woods. It was a poor little hut, but the man and woman there made them welcome. The woman gave them meat pie and buttermilk. The man made them a straw bed in the barn.

"This is good luck," said Magnus.

The next day there was more good luck. While they rested under a tree, a little gray donkey came up to them. She tried to put her nose into Magnus' pocket.

"She wants some of my wheat," he said, and he gave her a handful.

When they started on, she followed them. They could not drive her away.

"She must be lost," said Shan.

"Yes, and she may be a long way from home." Magnus patted the donkey's neck. "Do you want to belong to someone? Do you want to belong to me?" He climbed up on the donkey's back.

"She might throw you off," said Shan. But the donkey went quietly along.

"This is better than walking," said Magnus. He

found a long grapevine. He tied one end of it around the donkey's head and held the other end in his hand. "Now I can guide her," he said.

He and Shan took turns riding. The road grew steep and rough. Toward evening they looked out across a plain. Beyond was the sea.

A mist had come in from the sea. Far away were roofs and towers rising out of the mist. They shone red and gold in the evening light.

Shan stopped and pointed. "There it is, Magnus! There is Camelot!"

King Arthur

Late that night Shan and Magnus came to the walls of Camelot. Many others were there. Some had built cook-fires. Some had put up small tents.

A few horses and donkeys were tied outside the gate. Magnus tied his donkey with them.

A man told Shan, "We are waiting until morning. The gate will open then, and we can go into the city."

Shan and Magnus waited with them. They listened to the people talking. Some had come to the city to find work. Some had come to beg. Others, like Shan, had come to see the King.

The night passed quickly. In the morning the gate was opened. Leading the donkey, Shan and Magnus went into the city.

"Magnus, look!" said Shan.

"Eh! I never thought it would be like this," said Magnus.

They had not known a city could be so beautiful. The streets were of smooth stone. Beside each house was a garden of trees and flowers. In one garden they saw a peacock with its tail feathers opened like a great fan.

They walked up a street and through a market place. They passed many people on the way. Children were playing beside a fountain. Men and women were going in and out of shops.

"Lords and ladies all around us!" said Magnus. "They'll not believe me when I talk of this at home."

They came to King Arthur's castle. The walls and towers were of smooth white stone. For a long time Magnus looked up at the towers. "They look as high as the sky," he said.

Guards walked back and forth before the castle gate. Shan spoke to one of them. "I have come to see the King."

"On two special days each month he sees the people," the guard told him. "You must wait for the next special day."

"When will that be?" asked Shan.

"In six days more," said the guard.

Shan and Magnus looked at each other. "What shall we do while we wait?" asked Magnus. Shan shook his head.

They walked slowly back to the fountain. They stopped there for a drink, and the donkey drank too.

A man came by. He asked Magnus, "Is that your donkey?"

"Yes, sir," said Magnus.

"I am a woodman," said the man. "I need someone to work for me. Will you bring your donkey and help me carry firewood into the city?"

"Yes, sir, I'll work for you," said Magnus.

"Do you need me too?" asked Shan.

"No," said the man, "but there is work in Camelot for boys like you. If you look, you can find it."

Shan looked about the market place. He asked for work at a baker's. The baker sent him to a tailor. The tailor sent him to a shoemaker.

The shoemaker gave him work. "Carry the water and wood, and sweep the floor," he said, "and I'll give you food and a place to sleep."

So Shan worked for five days for the shoemaker. On the sixth day he went to the castle.

The gate was open. He went into the courtyard. He waited there with all the others who had come to see the King.

Many of the people were dressed in silk and fine linen. Shan was still in his goatskin clothes. He wished he had something better to wear before the King.

He heard someone say, "Here comes a knight of King Arthur."

Someone else said, "Yes, it is Sir Kay."

The knight came out across the courtyard. He

was straight and tall, and his head was held high. He said in a sharp voice, "Stand in a line, all who wish to see the King. I shall let you in one at a time."

The people stood in a line.

Sir Kay looked at Shan. "Why are you here?"

"To see the King, Sir Knight," said Shan.

"This is no place for children who wish to look at the King," said Sir Kay.

"I wish to do more than look at the King," said Shan. "I have come a long way and waited a long time to speak to him."

"What do you wish to say?" asked Sir Kay.

"That is for the King to hear," said Shan.

Another man had come out into the courtyard. He looked much younger than Sir Kay. He had a friendly face.

"The boy has his rights, Kay," he said.

"This is nothing to you, Gareth," said Sir Kay.

"Let us not quarrel," said the other man.

Sir Kay said no more to Shan. He went to the castle door and began to let the people in to see the King.

All day Shan stood in the courtyard. When no one else was left, Sir Kay called him into the castle.

Shan waited in a small room. There was a curtain across the doorway. He looked out through the curtain into a great hall.

At the end of the hall he saw a round table. It was the largest table he had ever seen. All around it were chairs — more than a hundred, he thought. On each chair was a name.

He knew that this must be the Round Table where King Arthur sat with his knights. He wanted to go nearer. He wanted to look at the names on the chairs. As he started out into the hall, he heard Sir Kay's voice.

"There is one left, Your Majesty," said Sir Kay. "He is only a boy in goatskin clothes, and I think he has nothing much to say. If you wish, I shall send him away."

"Bring him before me," said another voice.

Shan's heart beat faster. He knew that he had heard the King.

Sir Kay came back to the little room. "His Majesty will see you," he said.

Shan went out into the great hall where a man sat on a throne.

He saw the man's velvet robe and the gold crown on his head. He looked into the man's face, and it was a kind face, with eyes that were kind and a little sad.

"Kneel before the King!" whispered Sir Kay.

Shan knelt.

"Rise," said King Arthur.

Shan stood before the King. "I thank Your Majesty, and I beg you to hear me."

"I will hear you," said the King.

"I am Shan, the son of Lord Weldon. Once I lived in Weldon Castle with my father and mother. My uncle came — a wicked man. He took my father hunting, and my father was never seen again. My mother and I ran away to save ourselves. Now my uncle lives in the castle that should be mine."

The King sat for a while with his chin in his hand.

"If this is true, a great wrong has been done," he said. "You shall have a knight to go with you to Weldon Castle. But I do not know which it will be. I have already sent most of my knights to far places."

A man came out of a room behind the throne.

"Your Majesty," he said, "I am here."

Shan saw that it was the young knight he had seen in the courtyard.

"You, Sir Gareth?" said the King. "Were you not wounded when you last rode in the hunt?"

"That was a week ago, and my wound has healed," said Sir Gareth. "If it pleases Your Majesty, I will ride with the boy."

And he looked at Shan and smiled.

Sir Gareth

The next day they rode out from Camelot —
Sir Gareth, Shan, and Magnus.

Sir Gareth led the way on his black war horse.
Shan rode behind him on a brown pony from
the King's stables. He carried Sir Gareth's shield.
Magnus rode his donkey behind Shan. He car-

ried Sir Gareth's lance. It was a lance of the finest ashwood with a tip of steel, and it was twice as long as the donkey.

They rode through woods and up steep hills and down. It was hard for them to talk with one another then. But every evening, when they stopped for the night, Sir Gareth told stories.

He told of King Arthur and the beautiful Queen Guinevere. He told of Merlin the wise man and Lancelot, one of the greatest of all knights.

"How can a boy grow up to be a knight of the Round Table?" asked Shan.

"A boy like you?" asked Sir Gareth.

"Yes, a boy like me," said Shan.

"I have something to tell you — something you may like to hear," said Sir Gareth. "Before we left Camelot, King Arthur spoke to me of you."

"Of *me*?" said Shan.

"Yes. He said, 'I like the way the boy stands and looks me in the eye. If his story is true, it may be that we can make a place for him here at the castle.'"

"Did he — did he mean that I might be a knight?"

"I can tell you this much," said Sir Gareth. "The King likes to find his knights when they are young. First they are page boys at the castle. They wait on the table and work in the kitchen. When a page boy is older, he is made a squire. A squire helps the knights with the horses and armor."

"And after that he is made a knight?" asked Shan.

"Yes, if he has learned his lessons well."

"Sir Gareth, do you think the King *will* call me to Camelot some day?" asked Shan.

"If your story is true," said the knight, "I think he may."

"I have told the truth," said Shan. "You will see that I have."

One morning Shan saw the walls and towers of Weldon Castle.

He pointed. "There is my home."

Sir Gareth nodded. He rode on faster than ever.

They came to the castle gate. A watchman called down from the wall, "Who is there?"

"A knight of King Arthur, come to see your lord," Sir Gareth called back.

After a little while the watchman said, "My lord will see you, Sir Knight."

Sir Gareth, Shan, and Magnus rode into the courtyard.

Lionel came out of the castle. He was dressed in fine linen and a velvet robe.

"Welcome, Sir Knight," he said, with a smile.

Sir Gareth did not smile. "Are you Lord Lionel?" he asked.

"I am, and this is my castle," said Lionel.

"I come from the King," said Sir Gareth. "I come here to right the wrong done to this boy."

Lionel looked at Shan. "Who is this boy?" he asked.

"You know me well!" said Shan.

"But I do not," said Lionel. "Tell me your name."

"I am Shan, and you knew me as soon as I came through the gate."

"Shan? Shan? I know the name," said Lionel.

"It was the name of my brother's son. But he is dead. Last year he and his mother went away into the woods and were killed by wolves."

"You can see I was not killed by wolves, and neither was my mother," said Shan. "How can you look me in the face after what you have done? First you took my father from me. Then you took my home—"

"I will hear no more of this," said Lionel in anger. "The son of my brother is dead. This boy is in a wicked plot to steal my castle from me. Take him out of my sight!"

Sir Gareth looked at Shan. "Can you prove that you are Shan and what you say is true?"

"Yes, I can prove it. There are people here who know me."

Sir Gareth said to Lionel, "Bring everyone out. Let us see if anyone knows the boy."

"Now we shall see," said Shan.

"Yes," said Lionel, "we *shall* see."

The Field of Battle

All Lionel's men and all his servants came into the courtyard. They walked past Shan and looked at him. They said, one after another, "I do not know this boy."

"Some of them *do* know me!" said Shan. "They are afraid to speak." He saw a white-haired man by the wall. "There is my friend Nappus," he said. "He will know me."

He jumped down off the pony and ran across the courtyard. "Nappus, I've come home!"

The old man came to meet him. He caught Shan by the hand and knelt before him.

"You see — Nappus knows me," Shan said to Sir Gareth.

"This man's name is not Nappus," said Lionel. "He has no name. He is only a poor madman who can neither hear nor speak nor tell one face from another. I let him stay here only because I am sorry for him. Take him away."

Two servants took Nappus by the arms and led him back to the wall.

Shan stood before Sir Gareth. "Believe me, Sir Knight, I have told the truth."

"Believe him not, Sir Knight," said Lionel. "He has never set foot inside these walls before."

"This was my home," said Shan.

Sir Gareth's eyes were troubled. "Can you prove what you say?"

Shan did not answer. He did not know what to say.

"He can prove nothing," said Lionel.

A wind blew across the courtyard. A few leaves blew about Shan's feet. They were oak leaves. He looked up quickly. He saw the garden and the old oak tree. He said, "I can prove everything!"

He went into the garden. Lionel and Sir Gareth followed him.

Shan climbed into the oak tree. He felt among the leaves and branches. He found the hollow in the tree trunk.

He felt inside the hollow. His hand touched nothing but sticks and leaves.

Lionel shouted from below, "Come down from my tree! Why do you climb it?"

Shan put his hand farther into the hollow. His fingers touched smooth wood. It was the corner of a box.

He lifted out the box. There was a rope around it — the one he had tied there long ago. With the rope about his shoulders and the box on his back, he climbed down.

"This box I hid in the tree before I went

away," he said. "I alone knew where it was. In it is my father's sword."

He opened the box. He took out his father's sword and held it high.

"The sword is mine!" cried Lionel. "It is mine, I tell you!" There was hate in his eyes, as he started toward Shan.

Sir Gareth moved between them. "Now I know the truth," he said to Lionel. "You will fight me, not the boy."

On the field below the castle wall, Lionel and Sir Gareth waited face to face. They were on horseback. Each was ready with lance and shield.

On one side of the field were Lionel's men. On the other side were Shan and Magnus.

One of Lionel's men held a handkerchief high and let it fall. It was the signal for the fight to begin.

The horses charged. They met in the middle of the field. Lionel's lance broke against Sir Gareth's shield. Sir Gareth fell from his saddle.

But Lionel's shield had been struck too.

"Eh! They're both on the ground. Sir Gareth —
quick!" shouted Magnus. "He's coming at you with
his sword!"

Sir Gareth was on his feet. He drew his sword
just as Lionel sprang upon him. Their swords
clashed together, and Sir Gareth moved back.

"He's hurt," said Magnus.

"He had a wound when we rode from Camelot," said Shan.

He and Magnus cried out as Sir Gareth fell to
his knees. Lionel lifted his sword in both hands.
The blade flashed as he brought it down.

But Sir Gareth had thrown himself out of the way. Lionel's sword went deep into the ground. Before he could draw it out, Sir Gareth had the point of his sword at Lionel's throat.

"Will you yield?" he cried.

Lionel stood like a rock.

"Will you yield?" Sir Gareth cried again.

Slowly Lionel bowed his head. "I yield," he said. He gave up his sword.

Sir Gareth spoke so that all could hear, "You and your men will ride at once to Camelot. You will tell King Arthur that Sir Gareth sent you. The King will do with you as he wishes. The servants are not to blame. They may stay."

He and Shan and Magnus went up the hill to the castle. They went into the great hall where Shan had left his father's sword.

Shan took the sword up in his arms. He looked down at it for a little while. Then he held it out to Sir Gareth.

"I give you this, Sir Knight," he said. "I give it with my thanks."

Sir Gareth shook his head. "I have one sword,

I have no need for two. No, the sword is yours—"
He stopped. He leaned back against the table.

"Are you hurt?" asked Shan.

"No," said Sir Gareth, "but I must rest." Shan
and Magnus helped him to a bedroom. He lay
down.

"Let me bring Nappus to you. He is a good
doctor," said Shan.

When he went out into the great hall, he found
Nappus already there.

The old man's eyes were bright with excitement. He made a sign for Shan to follow him.

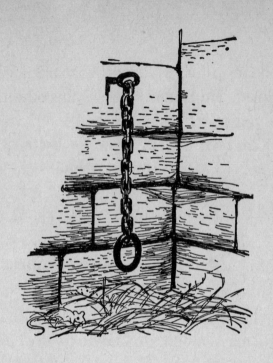

The Dungeon

Shan went with Nappus through a doorway. Now he saw that the old man had a torch in one hand and a key in the other.

Nappus lighted the torch. He opened an iron door in the floor and started down a stairway.

It was the way to the dungeon.

Shan stopped. He began to think that what Lionel had said might be true. He began to fear the old man had really gone mad.

Again Nappus made a sign for Shan to follow. Shan followed him down the stairs.

Nappus unlocked a door and threw it open. Shan looked into a room in the dungeon. In the light of the torch he saw a man lying on the floor. The man was thin. His hair and beard were long. His clothes were in rags.

He did not turn his head. "Who is it?" he said. "What do you want with me?"

Shan stood very still. He knew that voice.

He cried out, "Father!"

The man looked up "Shan! . . . Shan, it *is* you!" He began to weep. "My poor boy, now you are a prisoner too."

"No, Father—"

"Tell me of your mother, Shan. Tell me quickly. Is she safe?"

"She is safe. She will soon be here." Shan could hardly speak. He could not move from the doorway.

"Why do you stand and look at me so?" asked his father. "Are you afraid?"

"No," said Shan, "but I — I thought— "

"I know," said his father. "You thought I was dead."

"Yes," whispered Shan.

"On that day of the hunt, your uncle meant to kill me," said his father. "But I looked into his face, and he was afraid and put his sword away. For a while he kept me prisoner in the woods. Then he brought me to my own dungeon. He thought I would die here."

Shan went to his father. He put his arms about him and tried to lift him from the floor. "Now you are free."

"Free? Where is my brother?" asked Lord Weldon. "Where are his men?"

"They are gone," said Shan. "They can do us no more harm."

"But how can that be?" asked Lord Weldon.

"I'll tell you. When we are out of this place, I'll tell you everything," said Shan. "Here, let me help you up the stairs."

"I must close my eyes at first," said Lord Weldon. "The sun will be too bright."

He put his hand on Shan's arm. Slowly they climbed the steps, while Nappus went ahead, holding the torch to light the way.